AZTEC ATTACK

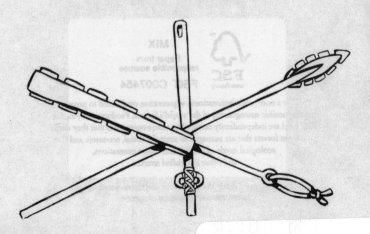

First published in Great Britain by HarperCollins Children's Books in 2014
HarperCollins Children's Books is a division of HarperCollinsPublishers Ltd,
77-85 Fulham Palace Road, Hammersmith, London, W6 8JB.

The HarperCollins website address is: www.harpercollins.co.uk

1

Text © Hothouse Fiction 2014
Illustrations © HarperCollins Children's Books 2014
Illustrations by Dynamo

ISBN 978-0-00-755004-3

Printed and bound in England by Clays Ltd, St Ives plc

FSC™ i   nal organisation established to promote
the resp   management of the world's forests. Products carrying the
FSC lab   are independently certified to assure consumers that they come
fro   forests that are managed to meet the social, economic and
            ecological needs of present and future generations,
            and other controlled sources

Find out more about HarperCollins and the environment at
www.harpercollins.co.uk/green

CHRIS BLAKE

TiME HUNTERS

AZTEC ATTACK

HarperCollins *Children's Books*

Travel through time with Tom
on more

adventures!

Gladiator Clash

Knight Quest

Viking Raiders

Greek Warriors

Pirate Mutiny

Egyptian Curse

Cowboy Showdown

Samurai Assassin

Outback Outlaw

Stone Age Rampage

Mohican Brave

Aztec Attack

For games, competitions and more visit:

www.time-hunters.com

CONTENTS

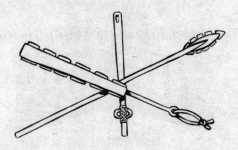

With special thanks to Martin Howard

PROLOGUE

1500 AD, Mexico

As far as Zuma was concerned, there were only two good things about being a human sacrifice. One was the lovely black pendant the tribal elders had given her to wear. The other was the little Chihuahua dog the high priest had just placed next to her.

I've always wanted a pet, thought Zuma, as the trembling pup snuggled up close. *Though this does seem like an extreme way to get one.* Zuma lay on an altar at the top of the Great Pyramid. In honour of the mighty Aztec rain god, Tlaloc, she'd been painted bright blue and wore a feathered headdress.

The entire village had turned out to watch the slave girl being sacrificed in exchange for plentiful rainfall and a good harvest. She could see her master strutting in the crowd below, proud to have supplied the slave for today's sacrifice. He looked a little relieved too. And Zuma couldn't blame him. As slaves went, she was a troublesome one, always trying to run away. But she couldn't help it – her greatest dream was to be free!

Zuma had spent the entire ten years of her life in slavery, and she was sick of it. She knew she should be honoured to be a sacrifice, but she had a much better plan – to escape!

"Besides," she said, frowning at her painted skin, "blue is not my colour!"

"Hush, slave!" said the high priest, Acalan, his face hidden by a jade mask. "The ceremony is about to begin." He raised his knife in the air.

"Shame I'll be missing it," said Zuma. "Tell Tlaloc I'd like to take a *rain* check." As the priest lowered the knife, she pulled up her knees and kicked him hard in the stomach with both feet.

"*Oof!*" The priest doubled over, clutching his belly. The blade clattered to the floor.

Zuma rolled off the altar, dodging the other priests, who fell over each other in their attempts to catch her. One priest jumped into her path, but the little Chihuahua dog sank his teeth into the man's ankle. As the priest howled in pain, Zuma whistled to the dog.

"Nice work, doggie!" she said. "I'm getting

out of here and you're coming with me!" She
scooped him up and dashed down the steps
of the pyramid.

"Grab her!" groaned the high priest from
above.

Many hands reached out to catch the slave
girl, but Zuma was fast and determined.
She bolted towards the jungle bordering
the pyramid. Charging into the cool green
leaves, she ran until she could no longer hear
the shouts of the crowd.

"We did it," she said to the dog. "We're free!"

As she spoke, the sky erupted in a loud rumble of thunder, making the dog yelp. "Thunder's nothing to be scared of," said Zuma.

"Don't be so sure about that!" came a deep voice above her.

Zuma looked up to see a creature with blue skin and long, sharp fangs, like a jaguar. He carried a wooden drum and wore a feathered headdress, just like Zuma's.

She knew at once who it was. "Tlaloc!" she gasped.

The rain god's bulging eyes glared down at her. "You have dishonoured me!" he bellowed. "No sacrifice has ever escaped before!"

"Really? I'm the first?" Zuma beamed

with pride, but the feeling didn't last long. Tlaloc's scowl was too scary. "I'm sorry!" she said quietly. "I just wanted to be free."

"You will *never* be free!" Tlaloc hissed. "Unless you can escape again…"

Tlaloc banged his drum, and thunder rolled through the jungle.

He pounded the drum a second time, and thick black clouds gathered high above the treetops.

"This isn't looking good," Zuma whispered. Holding the dog tightly, she closed her eyes.

On the third deafening drum roll, the jungle floor began to shake and a powerful force tugged at Zuma. She felt her whole body being swallowed up inside… the drum!

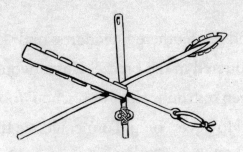

CHAPTER 1

KICK-OFF

Tom was trying hard to keep a football in the air with his feet. The final of the five-a-side tournament was due to start soon. His Townbridge team-mates were warming up, taking turns to strike practice shots at the goal. At the other end of the pitch, their Riverside School opponents were doing stretching exercises in front of their coach.

As Tom flicked the ball into the air, Zuma watched him curiously. Her face was painted blue, and her feathered headdress and white robes fluttered in the breeze. Zuma would have been a strange sight at a school football match. However, only Tom could see the slave girl, and Chilli her little Chihuahua, who was scampering around, yapping excitedly.

Zuma folded her arms. "This is a silly game," she said. "The Aztec game of Ulama is much better. The goal is smaller – just a stone hoop instead of that great big net. Plus the players use their hips to knock the ball around. It's very skilful. Why do you use your feet?"

Tom glanced at her. "It is called *foot*ball," he said. "The clue's in the name." Distracted, he lost control of the ball. He sighed as it bounced across the pitch, with Chilli chasing after it.

"Are you sure you should be on the

team?" Zuma asked. "You're not very good at keeping the ball in the air."

"I was doing fine until you interrupted," Tom said. He jogged over and rescued the football from Chilli, who was sniffing it suspiciously.

"Tom!" Two voices were calling out his name from the sidelines. He turned to see his mum and dad waving at him.

"Good luck!" Mum shouted, clapping.

"Townbridge for the cup!" added his dad.

Tom waved back, giving his parents the thumbs up.

"Er, Tom?" Zuma called out. "The rest of your team is talking to that bald man."

Tom looked across. His team-mates had gone into a huddle round Mr Simmons, the coach. The match was about to start. "Uh-oh!" he said. "Better go."

As Tom walked away, Zuma ran over to the football he had left behind. Pulling back her foot, she kicked it as hard as she could across the pitch. Tom's eyes widened as he watched the ball sail through the air.

Smack! It hit Mr Simmons right on the back of his head.

The coach whirled round. "Tom Sullivan!" he shouted. "What do you think you're playing at?"

"It wa—" Tom started to say. Then he stopped. He could hardly tell the coach an invisible Aztec slave girl had kicked the ball… He looked down at his feet, his face burning with shame. "Sorry, Mr Simmons," he said. "It was an accident."

"I can't believe you're messing around now," said the coach. "As you can't take the game seriously, you can sit on the substitute's bench." He pointed to a bench next to the pitch.

Tom's face went even redder – how could this happen in front of his mum and dad? He nodded miserably and walked off the pitch. Zuma and Chilli trailed after him.

"I'm sorry, Tom," said Zuma. "I never meant to hit him, I promise."

Tom sat down and folded his arms, ignoring her. He watched as the two teams took their positions. A strong gust of wind had started up, whipping across the pitch. The referee blew his whistle and the match kicked off.

Immediately, Riverside went on the attack. But Tom wasn't watching the game. He was looking up at the sky, which was suddenly filled with dark storm clouds. Fat raindrops splattered on his head. Chilli growled.

"Oh no!" groaned the boy sitting next to Tom. "Rain! You know what that means. The pitch is going to get muddy."

But Tom knew what it *really* meant – Tlaloc, the Aztec rain god, was on his way. Since the day Tom had accidentally released Zuma and Chilli from the drum in his dad's museum, the three of them had been travelling through time, searching for six golden coins that Tlaloc had scattered through history. Now only one coin remained. If they found it, Zuma would win back her former life, and her freedom.

There was a loud "Oooh!" from the crowd as one of the Riverside players hit the post.

But Tom wasn't paying attention to the action on the pitch. He was watching Tlaloc's face appear in the storm clouds above. It wasn't a pretty sight. Two bulging eyes stared out from beneath a feathered headdress. Tlaloc opened his mouth to speak, revealing two rows of sharp, pointed teeth.

"Tremble, mortals!" Tlaloc's thunderous voice shook the ground. "You may have found five of my coins, but your adventure ends here. You will never find the sixth."

"Oh yeah?" Zuma rose to her feet.

"We've done it so far. This time will be no different."

"Zuma's right," said Tom. "Not even your horrible tricks can stop us."

Tlaloc's face twisted into a snarl. The rain poured down even harder. "Do not be so sure, little boy!" he roared in a vicious gust of wind that almost knocked Tom off his feet. "You have done well to survive this long, but I have saved the most difficult and dangerous test until last." The god's snarl turned into horrible laughter. "It spells certain doom!"

"You said that last time," muttered Zuma. Tom couldn't help grinning.

"Smile while you can, mortal!" bellowed Tlaloc. "Soon I will be the one smiling – at your pitiful screams and tears."

Tom opened his mouth to reply, but it was

too late. Tlaloc had gone. The rain eased, and a sparkling mist rolled across the football pitch. Tom reached out and grabbed Zuma's hand. Chilli barked and Zuma scooped him up. "Good doggie," she said, "it's all right, we're just going on another little trip."

The ground fell away beneath Tom's feet. Wrapped up in the twinkling mist, he began floating through the tunnels of time.

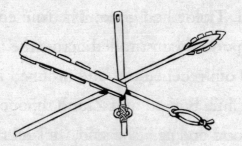

CHAPTER 2

RUMBLE IN THE JUNGLE

As they travelled back through time, Tom could feel his heart thumping in his chest. They had already gone to some very dangerous places, from the Wild West to the harsh Australian outback, but what was in store for them now? The god was cruel enough to send them anywhere – to the inside of a volcano, or the bottom of the ocean!

So he was relieved when the sparkling mist

faded and he felt solid ground beneath his feet. Tom looked round quickly, and gasped. It looked like some kind of paradise. There were tall trees everywhere and thick bushes of emerald green. Flowers blazed in every colour of the rainbow. A waterfall poured over rocks into a crystal-clear pool.

Tom wiped his forehead. Wherever they were, it was hot. He was already sweating.

Zuma squealed with delight. "My old clothes!" she said happily. "The jungle! I'm home!"

Tom turned to see Zuma dancing for joy. Chilli was scampering happily around her feet. The slave girl's headdress and blue paint had disappeared. Now she was wearing a loose white blouse with short sleeves and a white skirt, both with bright red bands sewn along the bottom. Her dark hair was loose and shining. Only the gleaming black pendant she always wore round her neck remained.

Zuma stopped dancing and looked at Tom. "Nice clothes," she giggled.

Looking down, Tom saw that his football kit was gone. Instead he was dressed in a blue cloak, with a white cloth wrapped round his waist like a short skirt. "Thanks," he said, blushing. He pulled the cloak round himself to hide his bare chest and legs.

"You'll get used to it," Zuma smiled. "It's too hot here in Mexico to wear lots of clothes."

Tom would have preferred a T-shirt and shorts, but Zuma was right – it was hot and steamy, even beneath the shady trees. "So we're back in Aztec times?" he said, looking around. "Cool!"

"Wait until you see one of our cities," Zuma replied. A dreamy look crossed her face. "There are pyramids shining beneath the sun, great squares…"

"…and human sacrifices," Tom reminded her. "It may be your home, but don't forget how dangerous it is. Tlaloc said it would be our toughest challenge yet." He pointed at the black stone hanging round Zuma's neck. "Let's ask your necklace for help."

Zuma's pendant was magical and gave them clues to where Tlaloc had hidden the coins. "OK," she sighed. "But it will only be another silly riddle."

Tom grinned. Unlike the Aztec girl, he enjoyed trying to work out the pendant's clues. He watched with excitement as Zuma held up the black disc and began chanting softly:

"Mirror, mirror, on a chain,
Can you help us? Please explain!
We are lost and must be told
How to find the coins of gold."

Tom and Zuma leaned over the pendant as ghostly white words appeared on the stone:

Find the city on the eagle's path;
Use the stream to escape a god's wrath.
Beware the man who bears a disguise;
A false face hides the ultimate prize.
When fur and feathers fight for control,
The ring of stone is your ultimate goal.
Climb up to the house of rain;
The flying spear will end your pain.

As the words faded away, Tom saw that Zuma had gone pale. "What's wrong?" he asked.

"For once I understand some of this," she replied softly. "I think the house of rain means Tlaloc's temple in the Aztec capital, Tenochtitlán. That's where I was nearly sacrificed."

During their adventures together, Zuma had proved her bravery over and over again. This was the first time Tom had seen her look nervous. Then again, it wasn't that surprising. The last time she had visited Tlaloc's temple, the slave girl had only just escaped with her life.

"Don't worry," Tom said. "I'll be with you this time."

Zuma smiled as Chilli jumped up, putting his front paws on her knee. "I know, little doggie, you'll be there too." She grinned at the Chihuahua. "And we got out together before, didn't we?"

"The sooner we find Tlaloc's coin, the sooner you won't have to worry any more," Tom said firmly. "So let's get started. The riddle said we have to find the city on the eagle's path. Any idea what that means?"

Zuma shrugged and said, "I got the bit about the house of rain, but the rest is gibberish to me. Anyway, you're the brainbox. I don't see why *I* should have to solve it all—"

The slave girl froze. Following her gaze, Tom saw that a nearby bush was rustling. He crouched down and peered through the leaves. A furry, cat-like creature was hiding in the undergrowth!

Tom gulped. He had read about the dangerous animals you might meet in the jungle. Without weapons, he and Zuma wouldn't stand a chance. As the bush rustled again and the creature emerged, he realised there was no time to run...

"Oh no," hissed Zuma. "It's a jaguar!"

They were going to be a big cat's dinner!

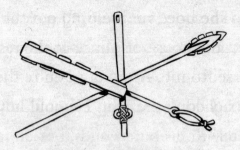

CHAPTER 3

CAT ATTACK

With a snarl, the creature burst through the bushes, pouncing on Tom in a blur of gold and black. Tom was knocked off his feet and pinned to the ground. He didn't even have time to cry out. He closed his eyes and waited for the jaguar to finish him off.

Instead, he heard the sound of mocking laughter.

Tom's eyes snapped open. It wasn't a cat sitting on his chest, but an Aztec boy about his age. The boy was wearing a cloak made out of jaguar skin. His fierce-looking helmet was made from the big cat's head.

Tom sighed with relief. He couldn't fight a jaguar with his bare hands, but another boy was a different matter. Gathering all his strength, Tom grabbed hold of his attacker and threw him off his chest, sending them both rolling across the ground. The boy was fast and strong, however. Before Tom could pin him down, he twisted Tom's arm up his back and pushed his face into the dirt. Pain shot through Tom's shoulder. He cried out.

"Hey, you!" Zuma shouted. "Leave my friend alone!"

There was a loud *thump*, and the grip on Tom's arm was suddenly released. Spinning round, he saw his attacker on his knees, rubbing the back of his head. Zuma had

a heavy branch in her hands, and looked
ready to swing it again.

The Aztec boy glared at her, anger
burning in his eyes. "You will pay for daring
to cross Zolin the Jaguar Warrior," he
snarled.

Thanks to Tlaloc's magic, Tom could understand every word Zolin said. It had been the same in every time period they had visited, even the Stone Age.

"You're not a Jaguar Warrior," Zuma said crossly. "They're noble Aztec warriors. They don't go around jumping on innocent travellers."

Zolin jerked his head at Tom. "He's no innocent traveller," he said. "Look at his pale skin and yellow hair! He must be a spy for some kind of enemy army."

"Don't be silly," snapped Zuma. "I'm a proud Aztec. Why would I travel with an enemy spy?"

"Good question," Zolin said slyly. "Maybe you're a traitor."

"What? How dare you!" Zuma lifted up her branch, ready to hit Zolin again. Then her eyes narrowed. "Wait a minute," she said. "An Aztec has to fight in two battles and capture twelve enemies before he's allowed to join the Jaguar Warriors. You don't look old enough to be carrying a sword."

"That's what you think," said Zolin, pulling a blade from its sheath.

Tom stared at the weapon. It didn't look like any sword he'd seen before. It was made of wood, with shards of dark glass stuck in its edges. The glass looked deadly sharp.

Zolin went into a crouch, holding his weapon ready to strike. Then he sprang at Zuma, his sword hissing through the air. She dived out of the way just in time. Tom scanned the jungle for something he could fight with. They were going to need more than tree branches to take on Zolin's sword.

At that moment, a spear came slicing through the trees. Zolin's eyes widened as it whistled beneath his nose before burying itself in a tree trunk with a loud *thud*. The shaft of the spear quivered in front of the Aztec boy's eyes.

"Your mother shouldn't let you play with swords," a voice said coolly. "You might get hurt."

Tom turned to see a teenager walk out from behind some trees. In one hand he held an odd–looking stick, in the other a shield decorated with feathers. He was wearing a feathered headdress that made him look like an eagle. Calmly, the boy walked over to Zolin and pulled his spear from the tree. "The first shot was a warning," he said. "Don't make me take another."

For a second, Zolin looked like he might

argue. He scowled at Tom and Zuma. "I won't forget you," he said, between clenched teeth. "You'll regret the day you crossed me." Then he fled into the trees.

The teenage boy turned to Zuma and Tom. "I'm Matlal," he said. "You can call me Mat."

"You're an Eagle Warrior!" Zuma replied. There was admiration in her voice. She turned to Tom. "Jaguar and Eagle Warriors are both special fighters in the Aztec army. But I've always thought that Eagles are the best."

Mat grinned. "I agree," he said. "Though I'm not a full Eagle Warrior yet. I'm still in training, though I'm much closer to finishing than Zolin. He's only just started and already he thinks he's a full-grown hero. He's got a lot to learn."

"Lucky for us you were here," Tom said gratefully. He pointed at the wooden pole Mat was carrying. "What's that?"

"You've never seen an *atlatl* before?" Mat asked. He sounded surprised. "Your people must be very primitive. Let me show you what it does."

He slotted his spear into the end of the wooden stick. "See that crooked tree down the path?" he asked, pointing.

Tom nodded. "Yes, but you'll never hit it

41

from here. It's too far away."

"That's what you think," Mat said. Raising his arm, he used the pole to hurl the spear along the path. It whistled as it flew away, impossibly fast. A second later it was quivering in the trunk of the tree Mat had pointed at.

Tom gasped. "Wow!"

Mat grinned. "The *atlatl* is like having the arm of two strong men," he said. "I came out to the jungle to practise with it. I was just heading back to the city when I saw Zolin causing trouble."

"Find the city on the eagle's path," Tom muttered to himself. Suddenly the riddle was starting to make sense. "Do you mind if we come along with you?"

Mat grinned. "Sure," he said.

"I'm Zuma, by the way," Zuma told him.

"My friend is Tom."

"Pleased to meet you both," said Mat. "We'd better get going. It's the harvest celebration tonight. I don't want to miss it."

When Mat went to collect his spear from the crooked tree, Zuma hesitated. "Tlaloc's temple is in the city," she said to Tom. "Do we really have to go? I'm already back home. Can't we just stay in the jungle and forget about the last coin?"

"If we do that, you'll never be free," Tom told her.

Zuma sighed. "I suppose you're right," she said. "And we've beaten Tlaloc five times already."

"He doesn't stand a chance against me and you," Tom said with a smile.

Mat had taken his spear and was already walking down the path. Zuma set off after him with renewed enthusiasm. "What are you waiting for?" she called to Tom over her shoulder. "Let's go!"

It was a long walk to the city. Tom and Zuma followed Mat along the narrow jungle path for what seemed like hours. The trees crowded in close as they ducked under creepers and clambered over roots. It seemed to grow hotter with every step. A thin mist gradually became a light rain. Before long, drops of rain were falling through the leaves above. In the distance, Tom heard a rumble of thunder.

"Tlaloc," Zuma muttered. "What's he up to now?"

"More of his tricks, probably," Tom replied. "We'd better hurry."

They started walking faster. The rain

turned into a heavy downpour, drumming on the leaves. Their feet squelched and slid in thick jungle mud. Tom picked up Chilli. The Chihuahua shivered and gave Tom's cheek a grateful lick.

"Careful," Mat shouted, coming to a stop. Tom and Zuma peered past him, shielding their faces from the rain. The path ahead narrowed, running along the top of a steep bank overlooking a small lake.

"That doesn't look very safe," said Zuma. "Isn't there another way to the city?"

Mat shook his head. "We're nearly there," he told them. "Follow me and I'll get you across."

But when the Eagle Warrior stepped on to the narrow trail there was a loud clap of thunder overhead, followed by a booming laugh. The bank collapsed beneath Mat's feet, sending him plunging down the slope to the lake below!

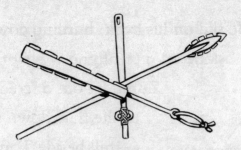

CHAPTER 4
CHUTE TO THRILL!

"Mat!" yelled Zuma, racing to the edge of the bank.

Tom followed after her, hoping they could pull the Aztec boy back up to safety. But Mat was tumbling down the slope towards the lake.

Just then, the edge of the bank crumbled. Tom and Zuma were caught up in the tide of mud flowing downhill. Tom desperately clawed at the churning goo, but it was no use.

He slid on his back, hurtling down the
slope on a terrifying wave of mud.
Zuma let out a scream
as she flew down the
hill beside Tom.
Trees flashed
past as
they picked
up speed.

The lake was getting closer and closer.

Then the bank came to a sudden end, and Tom tumbled over the edge. For a moment his arms and legs windmilled in thin air. Then he fell into the lake with a loud *splash*.

The water was dark with mud. Tom kicked upwards until his head broke the surface. Gasping for air, he looked around for Zuma. The Aztec girl was a few metres away, coughing and spluttering.

"Where's Mat?" she gasped.

"There!" yelled Tom, pointing at the Eagle Warrior.

Mat didn't look happy. He took a panicky gulp of air, and sank beneath the surface of the lake.

"Something's wrong!" Zuma shouted. "I don't think he can swim!"

Tom splashed over towards Mat. Diving down, he reached the struggling Aztec boy and gripped his arm. Kicking upwards, Tom dragged him to the surface just as Zuma arrived.

Mat was still spluttering and splashing his arms wildly.

"You're not going to drown," Tom told him. "Stop fighting me!"

Finally, Mat seemed to understand. His body went limp and he let Tom and Zuma pull him through the water. The three of them squelched ashore just as Chilli slid down the bank. The Chihuahua splashed into the lake and swam towards Zuma, his tail wagging with delight as he shook muddy water over her.

"Did you enjoy that, little doggie?" Zuma asked him.

"I think he wants to go again," laughed Tom.

Mat's face was serious. "You saved my life," he said. "I will never forget it, and I will give *my* life to protect you both. You have an Eagle Warrior's promise."

"It was nothing," Tom said modestly. "What are friends for?"

A smile flashed across Mat's face. He nodded.

Muddy and soaking, the three of them climbed slowly back up to the path. By the time they arrived at the main road, the rain had stopped. Clouds of steam rose from their clothes as they dried in the heat.

Soon they were looking down from the top of a hill at the capital city, Tenochtitlán.

Tom's jaw dropped. He had seen photos
of Aztec cities in his history books, but
they were all in ruins. This city was alive,
and massive – much bigger than Tom had
expected. It rose from an island in a vast

lake. Three long bridges connected it to the
shore. Just as Zuma had said, its pyramids
and buildings gleamed white beneath the
blazing sun.

As Mat strode ahead, Zuma held back. She looked thoughtful.

Tom looked at her. "How does it feel to be home?" he asked.

Zuma shrugged. "Since you released me from the drum, I've seen what a home is *really* like. You have so much, Tom – a family, a place where you belong. I don't even have a bed to sleep in. Even if we find the sixth coin, what will I do then?"

Tom walked beside her in silence. "Make a fresh start," he said after a while. "When we find that coin, you'll have the freedom to do anything you want with your life. Plus, you've only been back for a few hours and already you've made a new friend in Mat. *And* you have Chilli."

The Chihuahua barked in agreement, making them both laugh.

As they crossed one of the three bridges into the city, Tom looked around. The road was crowded with people arriving for the harvest celebration. Many had bright feathers in their hair and were wearing shiny gold jewellery. Merchants carried all kinds of food and fragrant spices, as well as luxury goods from all over the empire. Tom spotted one carrying a large sack of cocoa beans, while another merchant was balancing a towering stack of tortoiseshell cups.

Wherever Tom looked, people stared back at him. They didn't always look happy to see him. After a while Mat gave him a nudge. "Pull up your hood," he said. "Your yellow hair is making people suspicious."

Tom quickly did as he was told.

"YOU!" shouted a voice in the crowd. "Stop right there!"

Tom looked around, his heart in his mouth. A fat man in a feathered cloak was pushing his way through the crowd. Then, to his surprise, he realised it was Zuma that the man was glaring at, not him.

"That's Necalli," Mat whispered. "He's a slave trader and the brother of Acalan, the high priest of Tlaloc. What does he want?"

Zuma gulped. "Me," she said. "Necalli used to be my master. He offered me as a sacrifice to Acalan."

"We'd better get out of here," Tom whispered.

Zuma didn't need telling twice. She scooped Chilli into her arms and began running along the bridge. Tom and Mat pushed their way through the crowd after her.

"That girl's an escaped slave!" bellowed Necalli. "There's a big reward for anyone who catches her!"

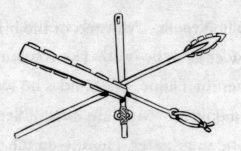

CHAPTER 5
TEMPLE TERROR

Tom's bare feet flew across the paving stones. Angry merchants hurled insults as he and Mat pushed their way past. Caged birds screeched and flapped their wings. Catching up with Zuma, Tom glanced over his shoulder. Necalli was puffing and panting – he was too fat to keep up. But his offer of a reward had worked. A furious mob now followed them in hot pursuit.

"This way!" yelled Mat.

They had reached the end of the bridge, and now entered the city. There was no time to look at the neat white houses – Tom and Zuma had to keep running as Mat led them through a maze of narrow streets. They turned left and right, over bridges, across canals. At every turn, the shouts of the angry mob could be heard.

"They're getting closer," panted Tom. "We'll never outrun them!"

"Down here!" Mat darted into an alleyway, immediately pulling Tom and Zuma into a doorway. Pushing Zuma behind him, the Eagle Warrior put his finger on his lips.

Wide-eyed, Tom stayed silent. All it needed was one person to spot them and they were done for. Seconds later, he heard yells and the sound of running feet.

Necalli's mob rushed past the entrance to the alleyway, barely glancing at the doorway. Gradually, the shouts disappeared. Tom slowly let out his breath.

"Phew!" said Zuma. "That was close! Thanks, Mat."

Although they were safe, Mat's face was grim. "On the bridge, you said you were an escaped sacrifice. Is that true?"

"Yes," replied Zuma. "I was going to be sacrificed to Tlaloc."

Mat looked shocked. "But sacrifices please the gods!" he said. "They die so we all might live. It's a great honour."

Zuma snorted. "It doesn't feel like an honour when the high priest is standing over you with a big knife in his hand."

"Tlaloc must have been angry when you ran away," said Mat.

"Tlaloc's *always* angry," interrupted Tom. "You could sacrifice every Aztec alive to him and he'd still be in a bad mood. You're not going to hand us over to Necalli, are you?"

Mat shook his head. "Whatever Zuma has done, I swore I would protect you. An Eagle Warrior does not break his word." He turned back to Zuma. "Is there anyone else who might recognise you?"

"Just Necalli," said Zuma. "I've only been to the capital once before, and that time I was covered in blue paint."

"And if we can find the special coin we need, Necalli can't do anything to hurt us," Tom told Mat. "We think it might be in Tlaloc's temple. Can you take us there?"

"Of course!" laughed Mat. "*Everyone* knows where Tlaloc's temple is. It's in the Sacred Precinct, in the middle of Tenochtitlan. Follow me."

Keeping watch, Mat led them deeper into the city. Tom made sure he kept his hood up, and Zuma stayed unusually quiet. The Aztec capital was a surprisingly clean city. Tom remembered from his history lessons that European cities at this time were ankle-deep in muck and rubbish. Tenochtitlan looked as if it had been scrubbed and polished that morning.

The closer they came to the centre, the more they were jostled by the crowds. The air was thick with the scent of food. Tom's stomach rumbled as he smelled spicy chilli and roasting corn. It seemed ages since he had last eaten.

Mat led them to a great gate guarded by Eagle Warriors. Spotting Mat's eagle headdress, they nodded at him and let them all through.

As they stepped into the Sacred Precinct, Tom gasped. The central square was enormous. Vast platforms and huge, stepped pyramids towered over him. Each pyramid was topped with a temple. At the centre of the precinct was a massive, open-air games court. Thousands of Aztecs were crowded inside the square, chattering excitedly. They were all facing the largest pyramid in the precinct, which had a squat building at its summit.

"That's the Great Pyramid," Zuma whispered to Tom. "Tlaloc's temple is right on top of it."

Men and women were hurriedly stepping backwards, creating a path through the crowd to the pyramid. An urgent murmur ran through the crowd: "The Shorn Ones are coming! The Shorn Ones are coming!"

Peering through the sea of faces, Tom saw a procession of tall warriors make their way through the square. The men were bald, except for a long plait of hair that covered their left ears, and their heads had been painted – half in blue, half in red or yellow.

"Who are they?" he asked Zuma.

"The Shorn Ones are the most feared of all Aztec warriors," she whispered back. "They have sworn a promise never to take a backwards step in battle, on pain of death."

The warriors certainly looked fierce, but it was the man leading them that interested Tom. His face was hidden in a deep hood,

and he was dressed in robes made of dazzling blue feathers. When Tom caught a glimpse of the man's face, he shuddered. It was ugly and twisted, coloured a glittering green.

Keep calm, Tom told himself, *it's only a mask*. Suddenly, he

remembered a line from the pendant's riddle:
A false face hides the ultimate prize…

"Who is that?" he blurted out, pointing at the masked man.

"Acalan, the high priest of Tlaloc," Mat hissed. "No more questions. People will know you're not an Aztec."

Tom bit his tongue. Instead, his eyes followed Acalan as the high priest began climbing the steps of the Great Pyramid. The Shorn Ones formed a ring round the base of the pyramid, giving the crowd warning stares not to come any closer.

"It won't be long until the ceremony begins," Mat murmured. "The high priest will sacrifice a human to make sure that Tlaloc is pleased. We will only eat well this year if Tlaloc blesses the harvest."

Tom couldn't hide his disgust.

Tenochtitlán might have been a beautiful city, but there were horrors lurking inside it.

Acalan paused on the pyramid steps and looked out over the crowd. Tom felt as if the high priest was staring straight at him and Zuma.

"What's he doing?" Mat whispered to Tom. "Why's he looking at us?"

"I don't know," Tom whispered back. "But let's get out of here before he decides to say hello."

The three of them turned and slipped away through the crowd. But Tom could feel the high priest's gaze burning into the back of his head as they went. He was sure that Acalan was about to call out "Stop!", or send his Shorn One warriors after them. So when they reached the edge of the crowd without any fuss, Tom sighed with relief.

Then he looked up, and cried out in shock.

Staring at him were rows of empty eye sockets. Hundreds and hundreds of human skulls were grinning at him.

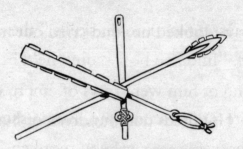

CHAPTER 6

GAME ON

Tom stumbled backwards, bumping into Zuma. "It's all right, Tom," she said. "They're just the skulls of old sacrifices. They keep them on a rack. It's called a—"

She was interrupted by mocking laughter. "Ha ha!" a familiar voice called out. "The yellow-haired spy is scared!"

Tom's head snapped round. Zolin, the trainee Jaguar Warrior, was standing nearby with a small crowd of sniggering friends.

"It's just a few mouldy skulls," the warrior sneered. "Imagine how scared he'd be in battle."

Before Tom could reply, Zuma shouted, "He's braver than you, you monkey-brained little twerp. He's fought assassins and killers. A mighty Japanese warlord once *begged* him to join his army."

"Japa-what?" Zolin howled with laughter. "I've never even *heard* of that kind of warlord, but he must have a pretty useless army."

"Get lost, you annoying insect," said Mat calmly.

"Leave it, Mat," Tom said, tugging Zuma's arm. "Come on, let's go."

"See?" jeered Zolin, jumping from one foot to the other in glee. "The coward is running away. If he were really brave, he'd

play in the Ulama game. The Jaguars are
playing the Eagles in a few minutes."

"What's he talking about?" Tom
whispered to Zuma.

"The Aztec game I told you about, remember?" she told him. "They often play a match before a sacrifice, to honour Tlaloc."

"Don't even think about it," Mat warned him. "Ulama can get rough. Players often get broken bones, or have their teeth knocked out."

Tom stared at the jeering Zolin. His blood was boiling. "OK, I'll play," he told the Jaguar Warrior. "And I'll win too."

But as Tom marched towards the games court, he realised he had made a big mistake. There were thousands of people jostling around, trying to get a better view of the action. What if one of them had been in the mob that had chased them through the city?

"Nice one, brainbox!" Zuma hissed in Tom's ear. "We're trying not to get spotted, remember?"

It was too late to back out now. Mat was already talking to the captain of the Eagle Warrior team, pointing at Tom. When he came back, his face glowed with excitement.

"It's all fixed," he said. "The Eagles will let you play. I told them it was a matter of honour."

The next few minutes passed in a whirl. Before he knew it, Tom was standing on the Ulama court. Thousands of eyes were staring at him.

An Eagle Warrior nudged him. "Keep the ball in the air," he said. "If you let the ball hit the floor, we lose a point. Every time we get it over the line at the Jaguars' end, we win a point. The first team to eight points wins, unless someone gets the ball through that hoop there –" he pointed to a stone hoop hanging from the side of a wall running the length of the court – "then their team wins immediately, but that almost never happens."

Tom gulped nervously. He'd never played Ulama before and he knew Zolin was out to get him. The young Jaguar was already giving him an evil-looking grin from the other end of the court.

"Wake up, Tom!" Zuma shouted from the sidelines. Tom had been so busy watching Zolin, he hadn't noticed that the game had started. The ball was flying towards him. With a heavy thump, it rocketed into his stomach.

"Ooof!" Tom dropped to his knees. The ball was made of solid rubber. It was like being kicked in the stomach by a horse. He groaned as it rolled away.

Zolin sprinted past as Tom climbed

painfully to his feet. "One point to us. Did that hurt, yellow-hair?" he mocked.

Seconds later, the ball was in play again. The Eagle team bounced the ball off their hips around the court to each other. But when Tom tried to copy them he found out just how difficult Ulama was. The heavy ball slammed into his hip at bruising speed. Tom tried to knock it in the direction of the nearest Eagle.

Instead, it shot away in a completely different direction — straight towards a Jaguar player.

The crowd groaned. His cheeks red with embarrassment, Tom spotted Zolin laughing hysterically. He gritted his teeth again.

If I can't play by their rules, I'll play by mine, he told himself.

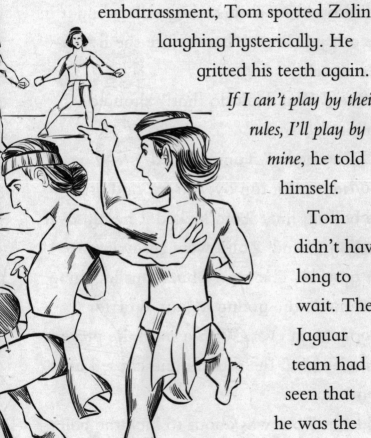

Tom didn't have long to wait. The Jaguar team had seen that he was the weakest player. Their next attack came straight towards him. This time, Tom was ready. As the ball came hurtling towards him, he caught it on his chest. Letting the ball drop to his feet, he began juggling it in the air, just like he had before the five-a-side match.

"Hey! You can't do that!" shouted Zolin.

"Watch me," Tom grinned.

When Zolin ran over to try and grab the ball off him, Tom kicked it neatly over the boy's head. Zolin went sprawling to the ground. The crowd burst out laughing. This made the young Jaguar Warrior angrier than ever. With a snarl, he picked himself up off the ground and chased after Tom.

Just as Tom was about to kick the ball

to an Eagle team-mate, Zolin crashed into the back of him. Tom staggered sideways, the ball skewing off his foot. Instead of flying to his team-mate, it looped up high into the air. Holding his breath, Tom watched as the ball bounced off the wall and dropped neatly through the stone hoop. The Eagle team had won!

For a second there was complete silence. Then everyone in the crowd was on their feet cheering. Eagle Warriors ran up to Tom. Laughing, they lifted him into the air and carried him back towards Zuma and Mat. The two of them were hugging each other at the end of the court. Chilli was running around their feet in excited circles.

Over the cheers Tom could still hear Zolin's whining voice. "But it's not *fair*!"

the young Jaguar Warrior was shouting.
"He used his feet!"

No one was listening. Even the other Jaguar
Warriors were offering congratulations.

"You were *TERRIFIC*!" Zuma yelled, as the Eagle Warriors dropped him back to earth. "See, I told you Ulama's a much better game than your silly football."

"The team wants us to join them at the Eagle Palace to celebrate," Mat shouted over the heads of the players. "There will be a feast in your honour, Tom!"

Tom's stomach rumbled at the word 'feast'. He could still remember the chilli he'd smelled on the street earlier. A grin spread across his face. "Sounds great – I'm starving."

"There will be tortillas and chocolate and roasted grasshoppers..." Mat's voice was lost in shouts, as the Eagle team crowded round Tom again, pushing him towards the exit.

Then, from somewhere behind him, Tom heard Chilli bark furiously.

"Let me go!" he heard Zuma shout.

Pushing his way back through the crush, Tom's heart sank. Necalli the slave owner had grabbed Zuma's arm and was marching her across the square. Zuma had warned Tom that she needed to stay out of sight. Now Necalli had her in his clutches, and it was all Tom's fault!

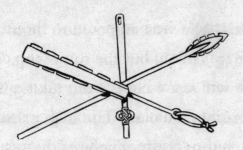

CHAPTER 7

EAGLES' NEST

"Leave her alone!" cried Tom. He ran over and stood in front of Necalli, blocking his way. "You're not taking her anywhere."

"And who is going to stop me, boy?" Necalli smirked.

"I will," said Mat, stepping out from behind Tom. He pulled his *atlatl* spear thrower from his belt. "The girl is under my protection. Now take your hands off her."

"The girl is an escaped slave!" Necalli

protested. "She was supposed to be a sacrifice to Tlaloc, but she ran away. This time she will not escape. I am taking her to my brother, Acalan. The high priest will sacrifice her as the highlight of the harvest ceremony tonight."

Necalli puffed himself up, expecting Mat to be frightened. But the Eagle Warrior didn't look impressed. "Zuma is under my protection," he repeated. "You will have to find another sacrifice."

By now the Eagle Ulama team had formed a circle round Necalli and Zuma. "If our brother warrior is sworn to protect the girl, we are *all* sworn to protect her," said one. The other Eagles murmured their agreement.

"We will not allow you to leave with Mat's friend," said another. "Let her go."

Necalli looked around at the grim warriors' faces. At last he let go of Zuma's arm. "This is not the end," he muttered, barging out of the circle. Then the slave owner vanished into the crowd.

For a few seconds no one spoke. Then a

smile crept over Mat's face. "So," he said, "who wants roasted grasshoppers?"

An hour later, Tom sat back and sipped a cup of hot chocolate. His stomach was full of corn tortillas and a delicious stew made from vegetables. He had tried one grasshopper to be polite, but he'd found it a bit too crunchy for his liking.

"Do you like the hot chocolate?" Zuma asked him.

Tom made a face. "It's not like the hot chocolate at home. It's more spicy than sweet."

"They put chilli in it," said Zuma. "You should be grateful – this is a real honour. Chocolate's *very* expensive. People even use it as money. A poor slave like me could never afford it."

"Are the Eagle Warriors rich then?" Tom asked. He looked around. The Eagle Palace was an enormous building. The walls were covered in beautiful painted carvings. Through a large open window he could see warriors practising in a large courtyard.

Zuma nodded. "Warriors are very important to the Aztecs. They have their own special schools. Everyone respects them."

"Especially the Eagle Warriors," said Mat. He pointed through the gateway to the men in the courtyard. "Do you see how well we fight?"

Tom watched the warriors outside sparring with wooden swords and shields. It reminded him of time travelling with the Egyptian princess, Isis. During their first adventure he had learned to fight with the same weapons at a Roman gladiator school. "I'd like to try that," he said.

"Fight an *Eagle Warrior*?" Zuma laughed. "Are you crazy? You'd be thrashed!"

Tom smiled. "Want to bet?"

Mat slapped him on the back. "That sounds like a challenge," he grinned.

Minutes later, Tom was holding a sword and a round shield. He swung the wooden sword for practice. It was light but deadly, its edge glittered with razor-sharp chips of dark glass.

"Let's see how well you fight then," Mat said, circling him.

Tom took up his position, remembering what he'd been taught in Ancient Rome. *Stay calm and relaxed*, he told himself. *Keep your balance. Focus on defending, but watch for an opening to attack…*

Mat's first blow came out of nowhere. Tom stepped quickly to one side. Dodging the blade, he swung his own at Mat's unprotected side. The Eagle Warrior raised his shield just in time. Tom's sword clattered against wood.

Frowning, Mat struck again. This time, Tom knocked his sword away with his own and pushed forward, striking towards Mat's stomach, but stopping before he cut him. "That would have been a nasty wound," he said, grinning.

Mat raised his eyebrows. "You fight well," he said. "Again."

Before long the other Eagle Warriors in the courtyard had stopped sparring and gathered to watch Tom and Mat fight. Mat won the next match, then Tom won again. The Aztecs whispered excitedly to each other

when Tom used some fighting tricks he'd
learned at gladiator school. They had never
seen them before. Even Zuma was impressed.
She jumped up and down, cheering when
Tom won again.

"Let's try some different weapons," said Mat after the fourth match. "I might stand a better chance!"

Tom almost laughed as they changed their weapons. Mat handed him a long spear with

a large flat head. *Fighting with it would be like fighting with a Roman trident*, he thought to himself. And he had been trained with that as well.

Sure enough, Mat found it just as difficult to beat Tom with the spear. Wiping sweat from his forehead, he said, "Maybe I can win with the *atlatl*. It's my favourite weapon."

This time, Mat was easily the victor. With the help of the spear thrower, every one of his spears hit the target. Tom's spears flew wildly across the courtyard, missing the target by miles. Chilli scampered after every spear, trying to bring it back in his mouth.

"Come back here," Tom told the little dog. "We're not playing fetch."

"What's 'fetch'?" asked Zuma.

Tom blinked at her. "Don't Aztecs play

fetch with their dogs?" he asked. "When you throw a ball or a stick, the dog brings it back."

"Never heard of it," replied Zuma with a shrug. "Most dogs here are raised to be food."

Tom looked down at the little dog and suddenly felt queasy. "You Aztecs are so weird," he said. Fitting another spear to the *atlatl*, he tried again. The spear wobbled down the courtyard. An old teacher had to jump out of the way to avoid being hit.

"You're useless. It's just like the boomerang in Australia all over again," said Zuma. "Let me try." Grabbing the *atlatl*, she hurled a spear down the courtyard. It flew straight and true, nearly hitting the centre of the target.

"Nice throw," said Mat approvingly.

"You'd make a good Eagle Warrior!"

He was interrupted by a young boy, who was dashing across the courtyard, calling out his name. "Mat! There's a message from the head of the school. He wants to see you right away."

"This sounds important," Mat told Tom and Zuma. "I'd better go. You stay here. I'll be back soon."

He strode out of the courtyard, leaving Tom and Zuma on their own. To pass the time Tom practised with the spear thrower. He threw until his arm ached, but still he struggled to hit the target. Zuma sat in the shade of a tree, playing with Chilli. An hour passed, then another. There was no sign of Mat. Afternoon was starting to fade; the sun sank lower in the sky.

"Where *is* Mat?" Zuma said impatiently.

"It's going to be evening soon. We need to find Tlaloc's coin!"

Tom was starting to feel uneasy. "Do you think something's happened to him?" he asked.

"I don't know," Zuma replied. "But I think we should find out." She grabbed a passing Eagle Warrior by the arm. "How do we get to the warrior school?"

They followed his directions, keeping a look out for Necalli. When they reached the school, Zuma hurried through the entrance gate. They spotted a young warrior in the halls.

"Hey!" Zuma shouted out. "Have you seen Mat?"

"His room's that way," the warrior replied, pointing down a long corridor.

Zuma and Tom ran down the corridor.

When they found Mat's room and pushed open the door, Tom's heart sank. The place had been turned upside down. It looked as though there had been a violent struggle. As he looked around, Tom noticed that the bed was shaking. He crouched down. A young boy was hiding beneath it, trembling with fear. It was the boy who had brought the message to the Eagle Palace. Slowly, Tom helped him out.

"What happened?" asked Zuma. "Where's Mat?"

"I d-don't know," the boy stammered. "I was asked to bring him to the school, but then the Sh-Shorn Ones came. They said that A-Acalan has chosen Mat to be the harvest s-sacrifice tonight!"

"Necalli!" hissed Zuma. "This is his work, I know it. Tom, we have to get to the Sacred

Precinct right now. They'll have taken Mat to Tlaloc's temple on top of the Great Pyramid."

"Hang on a minute!" said Tom.

"What?" Zuma said impatiently. "We don't have much time."

"I know," replied Tom. "But we can't just go running up to the temple and ask Acalan to give us Mat back. There are Shorn Ones guarding the bottom of the pyramid, remember? We need a plan to get past them. Something clever."

Zuma nodded slowly. "I think I have an idea…" she said.

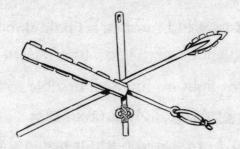

CHAPTER 8

STEPS OF DOOM

The streets of the capital were bright with blazing fires. People danced beneath flickering torches as hundreds of drums beat in time. The harvest ceremony had begun.

"Are you sure this will work?" asked Tom, as he and Zuma walked out into the street.

She nodded. "It's the best plan we've got."

Tom was wearing the armour and feathered helmet of an Eagle Warrior, a sword in one hand and a shield in the other.

The costume hid most of his pale skin and blond hair.

"In this light no one will be able to tell you're not Aztec," Zuma told him.

When Tom stared back at her, a shiver went down his spine. Zuma was wearing the robes of a human sacrifice again. Her skin had been painted blue. Colourful feathers shimmered round her head and the black pendant glistened at her throat.

Lifting her face, Zuma sniffed the evening air. "There's a storm on the way," she said. "Tlaloc is coming."

"Oh great, that's all we need," Tom groaned. "You know, since I first met Tlaloc I've never been able to understand why you Aztecs worship him. He's such a twit."

Despite the danger they were walking into, Zuma grinned. "Twit is *exactly* the right word for him," she said.

The Sacred Precinct was a sea of glimmering torchlight. Seeing Zuma's white robes and headdress, the people immediately made a path for her. Shouts of "May Tlaloc bless you!" and "Thank you for dying so we can live!" followed her and Tom. They stepped through the crowd, with Chilli following faithfully behind.

Thunderclouds were swirling around the temple at the top of the Great Pyramid. At its base, the Shorn Ones stood silent guard. Their painted heads looked monstrous in the firelight. Just looking at the fierce warriors made Tom gulp. But there was no time to feel nervous now. Mat's life depended on them.

Taking hold of Zuma's arm, Tom marched up to the bottom of the pyramid steps. A giant Shorn One stood in his way. "No one may pass," he boomed in a deep voice.

Zuma stepped forward. "Can't you see I am a sacrifice?" she snapped. "This Eagle Warrior is escorting me to the Temple of Tlaloc. It is my duty and honour to die tonight."

A look of confusion crossed the Shorn One's painted face. "The high priest has already taken the sacrifice up to the temple," he said.

"Didn't Acalan tell you?" said Tom. "He wants two sacrifices, to make sure Tlaloc gives us a bumper harvest this year."

"But if you're worried," Zuma added slyly, "why don't you go all the way up to the top of the pyramid and check with Acalan? Of course, I don't think the high priest will be very happy if the ceremony gets delayed. He might end up making *you* the second sacrifice instead of me."

"You may pass," the Shorn One said quickly, standing aside.

"Thank you," Zuma said. With her nose in the air, she stepped on to the staircase that led to the temple above. "Hurry up, guard," she shouted back at Tom. "I don't want to be late for my own death."

Tom had to stop himself from smiling. He knew Zuma loved playing a role. But when she pointed up the Great Pyramid a few seconds later it was no laughing matter. Acalan and Mat had reached the entrance to Tlaloc's temple. Mat was struggling hard in the high priest's grip, but he couldn't stop himself from being dragged inside.

Tom and Zuma raced up the pyramid after their friend, taking two steps at a time. Rain started to fall, splashing them with fat drops. In the distance, Tom heard a low growl of thunder.

The first set of steps led out on to a wide

terrace halfway up the Great Pyramid. As Tom and Zuma raced across the terrace, a figure dressed in jaguar skin stepped out from the shadows, blocking their path to the next set of steps. It was Zolin.

"Stop right there, yellow-hair!" he sneered. "You might be able to fool the Shorn Ones by dressing up like an Aztec, but I can see right through it."

"You again!" said Tom. "I should have known that you'd be mixed up in this."

"Acalan asked me to stand guard," Zolin said proudly. "He knew I wouldn't let him down." He drew his sword. "Ready to see how a *real* Aztec fights, yellow-hair?"

Tom stepped forward, raising his sword. He watched Zolin carefully. The young Jaguar Warrior was quick and strong, but did he know how to handle a sword?

He soon found out. Zolin lunged towards him, swinging wildly. Tom easily dodged the blow. The Aztec boy had no style at all. He used the sword like he was trying to chop down a tree.

"Come on, Tom!" called Zuma. "Give that jaguar fool a taste of your sword!"

Tom caught Zolin's second blow on his shield. With a crunch, the sharp glass shards cut into the wood. Quickly, he jumped backwards.

"Trying to run again, coward?" snarled Zolin. He swung his sword once more.

I'm not trying to run, thought Tom. *Just trying to get you off balance*. He lashed out with his shield. The blow smashed into Zolin's shoulder. He staggered backwards. *Just like that*, thought Tom.

Zolin's feet were slipping on the wet terrace. As he struggled to regain his footing,

there was a sharp bark and Chilli streaked
forward. With a snarl, the little dog sank his
teeth into the warrior's shin.

"Aaaargh! Get it off me!" screamed Zolin.
He raised his sword, ready to bring it down
on the Chihuahua.

He never got the chance. Tom stepped forward and swung his own sword in a mighty arc, knocking Zolin's weapon from his hands. The Jaguar Warrior watched in horror as his sword whirled away into the night, clattering on to the pyramid steps far below.

"You win, yellow-hair," snarled Zolin. "Finish me now." He closed his eyes and lowered his head.

Tom rolled his eyes. There was no way he would be 'finishing' anyone.

"You really are a little twerp," Zuma told Zolin. Running forward, she kicked the Aztec boy in his other shin. With a yelp of pain, Zolin half fell, half hopped away down the steps.

"That's for trying to hurt Chilli!" Zuma called after him.

They might have defeated Zolin, but he had cost them precious time. The storm was getting heavier. Wiping the rain from their faces, they dashed across the terrace. As they ran up the second set of steps, they heard Mat's voice shouting for help from inside Tlaloc's temple.

"Oh no!" Zuma cried. "We're too late!"

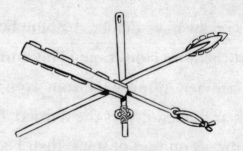

CHAPTER 9
HOUSE OF RAIN

The storm crashed over the Sacred Precinct.
Angry streaks of lightning crackled across
the sky. As he and Zuma reached the square
temple at the top of the pyramid, Tom
looked down. A sea of faces gazed up into
the flashing clouds. Even over the noise
of the storm, he could hear the whole city
chanting, "Tlaloc, Tlaloc, Tlaloc!"

A dark doorway led into Tlaloc's temple.
Fear gripped Tom. The last thing he wanted

was to go inside, but there was no choice. His friend was in danger. Judging by the look on Zuma's face, she was thinking the same thing. Taking a deep breath, they entered the temple at the same time. Their footsteps echoed off the walls as they sprinted along a gloomy passage. Up ahead, lights were blazing.

Tom and Zuma burst into a huge room lit by torches. A giant painted statue of Tlaloc glared down upon a stone slab in the centre of the room. Mat had been tied to the slab. His Eagle headdress, cloak and *atlatl* lay scattered on the floor. Acalan was standing over him, a knife in his hand. The high priest had thrown back the hood of his feathered robe. His jade mask gleamed in the torchlight.

Tom gasped. Embedded in the forehead of

Acalan's mask was a glittering gold disc. It was Tlaloc's last coin!

"Stop!" cried Zuma. "Get away from
him!"

Acalan turned. The evil-looking mask looked from Zuma to Tom. Then the high priest of Tlaloc chuckled.

There was a movement in the shadows behind Tom. Too late, he tried to run. A strong arm shot out and wrapped itself round him like a snake. Tom heard Zuma cry out, and saw that she had been grabbed too. Necalli emerged from the darkness. There was an ugly smile on his face. The slave owner was big and strong enough to trap both Tom and Zuma in an iron embrace. He laughed at Chilli as the Chihuahua snarled and snapped at his ankles. They had run straight into a trap!

"I knew you would try and save your little friend," Acalan sneered. "Why else do you think I took him?"

"You won't get away this time," Necalli told Zuma.

"*None* of you will get away," added Acalan, looking straight at Tom. "Tlaloc will have three sacrifices tonight. He will be very pleased. This harvest will be the best yet."

Acalan raised his knife into the air. Lifting his face towards Tlaloc's statue, he began to chant. On the stone slab, Mat was struggling to get free. Tom's eyes widened as he spotted a knot at the Eagle Warrior's ankle. It had obviously been tied in a hurry and was beginning to unravel.

Tom's mind worked quickly. If Acalan or Necalli saw that Mat might break free they'd stop the ceremony and tie him up more tightly. Tom had to do something to distract them...

"Hey, Acalan!" he shouted. The high priest stopped and looked at him, surprised. "I know something you don't know. In a few years ships will come across the ocean from Spain. The Spanish will conquer your people and destroy your empire. There will be no more human sacrifices."

"Silence!" hissed Necalli. "You must respect the high priest of Tlaloc!"

"Why?" said Tom. "I've met Tlaloc. He's nothing special. What did we decide he was, Zuma?"

"A twit," Zuma chipped in.

"That's right, a twit. No one will worship him after the Spanish arrive."

Both Necalli and Acalan gasped. Tom's plan was working. Mat had almost managed to get his foot free. He only needed a few more moments.

"Tlaloc will always be worshipped,"
Acalan howled. "He is the greatest god of
all!"

"That's what you think," said Tom.
"Tlaloc isn't—"

He didn't need to say any more. Mat's
foot was free. The young Eagle Warrior
kicked out, catching Acalan in the back of
the legs. The high priest stumbled forward
with a cry of surprise, tripping over Mat's
atlatl. As Acalan went sprawling to the floor,
the jade mask tumbled from his face.

"The mask, Zuma!" Tom said desperately.
"We have to get it!"

"Chilli!" yelled Zuma. "Fetch!"

Seeing where the Aztec girl was pointing,
Chilli sprang forward and grabbed the jade
mask in his teeth.

"Stop that dog, Necalli!" roared Acalan,

from his knees. "I need my mask to complete the sacrifice!"

The slave owner let go of Tom and Zuma and chased after Chilli. The Chihuahua bounded out of his reach.

"After him!" Acalan howled. His face was red with rage. "Quickly, you fool!"

Necalli scurried towards Chilli, but the little dog danced out of reach again. Grunting and lunging once more, this time Necalli let out a shout of victory. As the slave owner straightened up, Tom groaned. Necalli was holding Chilli by the scruff of the

neck, and easily wrestled the jade mask from his mouth.

"I have it, brother!" Necalli yelled. He held up the mask, shining in the torchlight. "It is safe!"

"Not yet, it isn't," said Tom.

Leaping over towards Mat's fallen weapon, he snatched it up and hurled it with all his strength. The spear flew across the temple and smashed into Acalan's jade mask, shattering it into a thousand pieces. As Tom punched the air in triumph, Tlaloc's gleaming gold coin went rolling away across the floor.

"Nooooo!" screeched Acalan.

"Nooooo!" screamed Necalli.

The two brothers dived for the coin at the same time. But Zuma was too fast for them. Covering the ground like lightning, she snatched up the coin and leaped out of the way. As Acalan and Necalli slid along the ground, their heads smacked together with a loud *crack*. They cried out in pain and fell backwards.

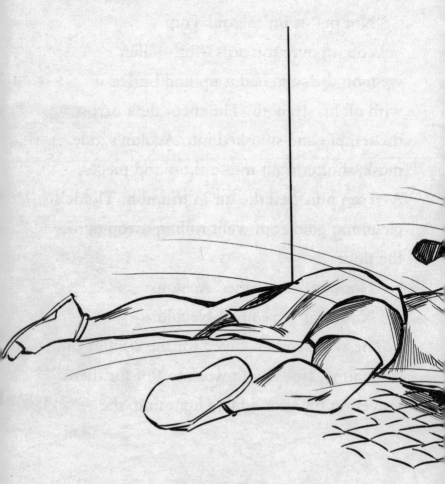

Zuma and Tom ignored them as they gazed in wonder at Tlaloc's last gold coin. Zuma's eyes were sparkling. They both grinned, and gave each other a high-five.

But as their hands slapped together, a rumble of thunder shook the temple. Rain began pouring from the ceiling. Tom and Zuma looked up into a face that was as furious as the fiercest storm.

Tlaloc had arrived.

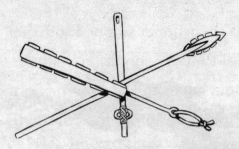

CHAPTER 10

FINAL WHISTLE

Tlaloc's face was full of rage, his eyes bulging out of their sockets. The rain god gnashed his sharp teeth together. Rain was hammering down on to the stone floor.

But Zuma was smiling from ear to ear. Without a word, she held up the golden coin. Then she flicked it up in the air to Tlaloc. For a long time the god said nothing. He looked almost too angry to speak. Tom held his breath. Would the god keep his word?

"You have passed all six of my tests," Tlaloc said eventually. "You have proved your courage. I shall take no more revenge on you for running away from your sacrifice. You have your life and your freedom. No one shall ever call you 'slave' again."

Zuma smiled. "Thank you, Tlaloc," she said.

Acalan and Necalli had picked themselves up from the floor, and were both rubbing their sore heads.

"You idiot, brother!" screeched Acalan. "Do you see what you've done? Now we'll never be able to sacrifice the girl!"

"*You're* the idiot!" Necalli snapped back. "If you hadn't—"

"ENOUGH!" roared Tlaloc. The two brothers immediately stopped bickering.

"Tom and Zuma have proved their courage, but you have only proved your stupidity. Now you will pay the price."

Two dark rainclouds separated themselves from the storm around Tlaloc and floated above Acalan and Necalli's heads, drenching the brothers.

"For the rest of your lives, a cloud of misfortune will follow you wherever you go," rumbled Tlaloc. "Even when others' crops flourish, your harvests will fail. Let it be a reminder of how you have let me down. Now get out of my sight."

Acalan and Necalli stumbled towards the exit of the temple, the clouds following their every step. The brothers knocked into one another in the doorway and then tripped going down the steps. Tom and Zuma giggled.

But Tom's laughter faded as Tlaloc turned
his bulging eyes upon him. He had to stop
himself from trembling. *I called him a twit*,
Tom reminded himself. *Twice!*

"Your time here is over," Tlaloc told him. "You may have helped Zuma win her freedom, but Tlaloc sees everything and hears everything. I will remember your insult. You had better hope our paths do not cross again."

White-faced, Tom nodded.

"Now prepare to return to your own time," the god told him.

"Can I say goodbye to Zuma first?"

Tlaloc paused. "Very well. You are insolent, but brave. As a reward I shall give you one minute."

In all the excitement, Tom and Zuma had nearly forgotten about Mat. Now they rushed over to the stone slab and helped to free the young Eagle Warrior. Mat sat up, rubbing his wrists. "You were right," he said to Zuma. "Sacrifice doesn't feel like much of an honour when the priest is standing over you with a knife."

"But you don't have to worry about being sacrificed any more," Tom added. "You're free now."

"I know," said Zuma. There was a sad look in her eyes. "I just wish I had somewhere to go."

"Come with me," said Mat. He jumped down from the stone slab and stood beside the Aztec girl. "You've saved my life twice now. I'd be honoured if you'd stay with me in my parents' house. I'm sure they'd love to have you." When Chilli jumped up at his knee, he added, with a laugh, "And you too, little doggie, of course."

Zuma's eyes lit up. "Really?"

Mat nodded.

"Great!" she said. "You could help me train to become an Eagle Warrior just like you!"

"I'm not sure Aztec girls are allowed to become warriors," said Tom.

"Ha! We'll see about that," said Zuma. "If I'm brave enough for Tlaloc, I'm sure I can be brave enough for the Eagle Warriors."

"If anyone can, it's you," grinned Tom.

A sparkling mist was swirling impatiently around Tlaloc's head. It was time to say goodbye.

"I have to go now," said Tom. "It's been a pleasure travelling with you, Zuma."

"You too," Zuma replied. "Thank you so much – you were *amazing*." She lifted the black pendant from round her neck and lowered the necklace over Tom's head. "This is so you remember me. You always were better than me at working out the riddles."

"Goodbye, Zuma," Tom said. Sadness welled up in his chest as Tlaloc's shimmering

mist began to close round him. With a loud
yelp, Chilli jumped into Tom's arms and
gave his face a big lick. "And goodbye to
you too, little doggie," laughed Tom, as he
scratched the Chihuahua behind the ears.

He put Chilli back on the floor and gave Zuma and Mat a final wave. Then the ground gave way beneath his feet, and Tom entered the glittering tunnels of time.

"Tom! Tom! You're up! Come on, there's only a minute left until full time!"

Blinking with surprise, Tom looked around. He was back at the final of the five-a-side tournament. Mr Simmons, his football coach, was staring at him with his hands on his hips. One of the Townbridge players was limping off the pitch with a twisted ankle.

Tom glanced at the scoreboard. The score was still 0–0! Leaping to his feet, he jogged on to the pitch.

"Go on, Tom, show them what you can do!" his dad shouted from the sidelines.

The referee blew his whistle. A second

later, Tom caught the ball on his chest and let it drop to his feet. One of the Riverside defenders rushed towards him – just like Zolin had on the Ulama court. This time Tom knocked the ball through the defender's legs and swerved past him. Out of the corner of his eye, he saw the referee look at his stopwatch and raise a whistle to his lips.

It was now or never. Pulling back his foot, Tom took a shot towards the goal. The ball flew through the air like a bullet, whistling past the Riverside goalkeeper into the back of the net.

The referee blew his whistle.

For a moment, there was silence. Then the crowd started cheering. Townbridge School had won the final! Tom was swamped by his team-mates. On the sidelines, his mum and dad were hugging each other and jumping with joy. Mr Simmons came over and slapped Tom on the back, telling him it was a great goal.

As his team-mates ran over and lifted him on to their shoulders, Tom felt something jangling round his neck – it was Zuma's black pendant, gleaming against his skin.

From far away in the distance there was
a small rumble of thunder. Tom smiled to
himself as he thought of the defeated Tlaloc,
and his friend Zuma, and the incredible
adventures they'd had. Then, for the second
time that day, he was carried off the pitch
into a cheering crowd.

TIME HUNTERS

TURN THE PAGE TO . . .

➤ Meet the REAL Aztecs!

➤ Find out fantastic FACTS!

➤ Battle with your GAMING CARDS!

➤ And MUCH MORE!

WHO WERE THE MIGHTIEST AZTECS?

Ahuizotl was a *real* Aztec. Find out more about him and other famous Aztecs!

AHUIZOTL was the eighth ruler of the Aztec Empire and one of the most powerful. Under his reign the size of the empire doubled. Ahuizotl was also responsible for rebuilding much of the capital, Tenochtitlán, including the Templo Mayor, the Great Pyramid with Tlaloc's temple on top of it. To celebrate the new temple Ahuizotl ordered 20,000 people to be sacrificed in its honour!

AZTEC
AHUIZOTL

Brain Power	280
Fear Factor	250
Bravery	250
Weapon: Macuahuitl	280
TOTAL	**1060**

MOCTEZUMA II was the ninth ruler of the Aztec Empire. When the Spanish explorer Hernán Cortés landed on the east coast of his empire, Moctezuma II invited him and his men to stay with him. But when the Aztecs and the Spanish fell out,

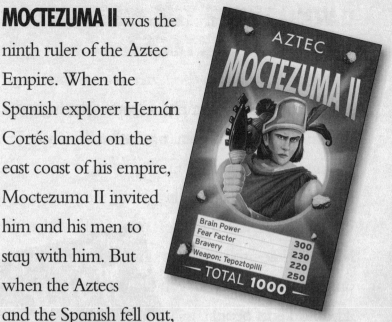

AZTEC

MOCTEZUMA II

Brain Power
Fear Factor 300
Bravery 230
Weapon: Tepoztopilli 220
250

TOTAL 1000

Moctezuma II became a prisoner in his own home. There was a huge battle during which Moctezuma II was killed, but the Spanish were forced to flee Tenochtitlán. However they joined forces with the Aztecs' local enemies and returned. The city eventually fell to the Spanish in 1521, which spelled the end for the Aztec empire.

TLALOC was the Aztec god of rain and the harvest. He was one of the most important and powerful gods in the Aztec world. Not only did he have a temple on top of the biggest pyramid in Tenochtitlán, but he had a whole mountain named after him.

Aztec people from all over the empire travelled to Mount Tlaloc to offer up gifts and valuables. Thousands of people were sacrificed in his name. With his bulging eyes and sharp fangs, the god was a terrifying sight.

AZTEC
TLALOC

Brain Power	
Fear Factor	340
Bravery	400
Weapon: Fierce Storms	360
	400
TOTAL	**1500**

ZUMA is an Aztec slave girl whose master
Necalli sold her as a human sacrifice to Acalan,
the high priest of Tlaloc. But
Zuma managed to escape
at the last second, along
with Chilli the Chihuahua.
Tlaloc was furious and
magically trapped the
pair in a drum for 500
years. When Tom
releases them, Zuma
is determined to win
back both her life
and her freedom.

She is brave and a fast runner – the
perfect ally for Tom as he travels through time.

WEAPONS

Ahuizotl fought with a maquahuitl! Find out about this and other weapons used by the Aztecs.

Maquahuitl: An incredibly deadly sword made from wood with flint or obsidian edges.

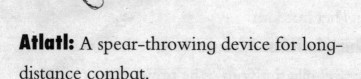

Atlatl: A spear-throwing device for long-distance combat.

Tematlatl: A sling made from fibres of the maguey plant used to hurl rocks great distances.

Quauhololli: A mace made of wood with a ball at the end, used to smash and crush.

AZTEC EMPIRE TIMELINE

In AZTEC ATTACK Tom and Zuma go to the AZTEC EMPIRE.
Discover more about it in this brilliant timeline!

AD 1100
The first
Aztecs
leave their
homeland
of Atzlan in
search of a
new home.

AD 1452
Tenochtitlán
destroyed by
a flood.

AD 1325
Aztec capital
Tenochtitlán
founded.

AD 1487
The new
Templo Mayor is
celebrated with
thousands
of human
sacrifices.

AD 1520
Moctezuma II killed.

AD 1522
The Spanish rebuild Tenochtitlán, calling it Mexico City and declaring it the capital of the Spanish colony of New Spain.

AD 1502
Moctezuma II takes the throne.

AD 1519
Spanish explorer Hernán Cortés arrives.

AD 1521
Tenochtitlán falls to Cortés. The city is destroyed.

TIME HUNTERS TIMELINE

Tom and Zuma never know where in history they'll travel to next!
Check out in what order their adventures actually happen.

10,000 BC–3000 BC
The Stone Age

AD 1427–AD 1521
The Aztec Empire

AD 1185–AD 1868
Feudal Japan

AD 1775–AD 1900
Era of the 'Wild West' in America

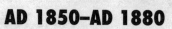

AD 1492–AD 1607
First contact between Native American tribes and European settlers in America

AD 1850–AD 1880
Bushranger outlaws become famous in Australia

FANTASTIC FACTS

Impress your friends with these facts about the Aztecs.

→ It wasn't just the Egyptians who built pyramids – the Aztecs did too. The Great Pyramid of Tenochtitlán was dedicated to Tlaloc, the god of rain and agriculture, and Huitzilopochtli, the god of war. It rose fifty metres above the city.
Wow, that's high!

→ The Aztec people worshipped many gods. The god Tezcatlipoca was believed to be able to turn into a Jaguar and see everything that ever happened. Every year a young man was sacrificed to him – by having his heart cut out!
That's quite a sacrifice!

➤ The Aztec capital was
called Tenochtitlán.
It was built on a vast
artificial island that
today is at the centre of
Mexico City. The location
was chosen when Aztec travellers saw
an eagle land on a cactus, an image
that had been predicted in an ancient
prophesy. *How eagle-eyed of them!*

➤ Chocolate played an important role
in Aztec rituals. Cocoa beans were
offered up as gifts to the gods by priests
and hot chocolate drinks were used in
ceremonies. *That's my
kind of ceremony!*

WHO IS THE MIGHTIEST?
Collect the Gaming Cards and play!

Battle with a friend to find out which historical hero is the mightiest of them all!

Players: 2
Number of Cards: 4+ each

→ Players start with an equal number of cards. Decide which player goes first.

→ Player 1: choose a category from your first card (Brain Power, Fear Factor, Bravery or Weapon), and read out the score.

→ Player 2: read out the stat from the same category on your first card.

➤ The player with the highest score wins
the round, takes their opponent's card
and puts it at the back of their own
pack.

➤ The winning player then chooses a
category from the next card and
play continues.

➤ The game continues
until one player has
won all the cards. The
last card played wins
the title 'Mightiest
hero of them all!'

AZTEC
AHUIZOTL

Brain Power	
Fear Factor	280
Bravery	250
Weapon: Macuahuitl	250
	280

TOTAL 1060

For more fantastic games go to:
www.time-hunters.com

BATTLE THE MIGHTIEST!

Collect a new set of mighty warriors — free in every
Time Hunters book! Have you got them all?

COWBOYS

- [ ] Wyatt Earp
- [ ] Wild Bill Hickok
- [ ] Buffalo Bill
- [ ] Billy the Kid

COWBOYS
WYATT EARP

Brain Power	
Fear Factor	300
Bravery	285
Weapon: Bullwhip	320
	330
TOTAL **1235**	

SAMURAI

- [ ] Lord Kenshin
- [ ] Honda Tadakatsu
- [ ] Lord Shingen
- [ ] Hattori Hanzo

SAMURAI
LORD KENSHIN

Brain Power	
Fear Factor	320
Bravery	280
Weapon: Katana Sword	320
	340
TOTAL **1260**	

OUTBACK OUTLAWS

- [ ] Ben Hall
- [ ] Captain Thunderbolt
- [ ] Frank Gardiner
- [ ] Ned Kelly

OUTBACK
BEN HALL

Brain Power	
Fear Factor	290
Bravery	300
Weapon: Bushranger Knife	380
	280
TOTAL **1250**	

STONE AGE MEN

- ☐ Gam
- ☐ Col
- ☐ Orm
- ☐ Pag

BRAVES

- ☐ Shabash
- ☐ Crazy Horse
- ☐ Geronimo
- ☐ Sitting Bull

AZTECS

- ☐ Ahuizotl
- ☐ Zuma
- ☐ Tlaloc
- ☐ Moctezuma II

MORE MIGHTY WARRIORS!

Don't forget to collect these warriors from Tom's
first adventure!

GLADIATORS

- ☐ Hilarus
- ☐ Spartacus
- ☐ Flamma
- ☐ Emperor Commodus

GLADIATORS
HILARUS

Brain Power	180
Fear Factor	250
Bravery	330
Weapon: Gladius	165
TOTAL	925

KNIGHTS

- ☐ King Arthur
- ☐ Galahad
- ☐ Lancelot
- ☐ Gawain

KNIGHTS
KING ARTHUR

Brain Power	340
Fear Factor	390
Bravery	270
Weapon: Broadsword	400
TOTAL	1400

VIKINGS

- ☐ Erik the Red
- ☐ Harald Bluetooth
- ☐ Ivar the Boneless
- ☐ Canute the Great

VIKINGS
ERIK the RED

Brain Power	305
Fear Factor	235
Bravery	260
Weapon: Axe	310
TOTAL	1110

GREEKS

- [ ] Hector
- [ ] Ajax
- [ ] Achilles
- [ ] Odysseus

PIRATES

- [ ] Blackbeard
- [ ] Captain Kidd
- [ ] Henry Morgan
- [ ] Calico Jack

EGYPTIANS

- [ ] Anubis
- [ ] King Tut
- [ ] Isis
- [ ] Tom

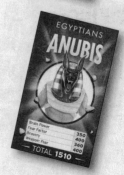

HAVE YOU READ THEM ALL...

Travel through time with Tom and Zuma as they battle the mightiest warriors of the past.

CHRIS BLAKE

TIME HUNTERS

FREE GAMING CARDS INSIDE

COWBOY SHOWDOWN
Battle the mightiest!

Got it!

CHRIS BLAKE

TIME HUNTERS

FREE GAMING CARDS INSIDE

SAMURAI ASSASSIN
Battle the mightiest!

Got it!

CHRIS BLAKE

TIME HUNTERS

FREE GAMING CARDS INSIDE

OUTBACK OUTLAW
Battle the mightiest!

Got it!

Got it!

☐

Got it!

☐

Got it!

☐

Tick off the books as you collect them!

DISCOVER A NEW TIME HUNTERS QUEST!

Tom's first adventure was with an Ancient Egyptian mummy called Isis. Can Tom and Isis track down the six hidden amulets scattered through history? Find out in:

Got it! ☐

Got it! ☐

Got it! ☐

Got it!

☐

Got it!

☐

Got it!

☐

Tick off the books as you collect them!

Go to:

www.time-hunters.com

Travel through time and join the hunt for the mightiest heroes and villains of history to win **brilliant prizes!**

For more adventures, awesome card games, competitions and thrilling news, scan this QR code★: